June 2003
WI

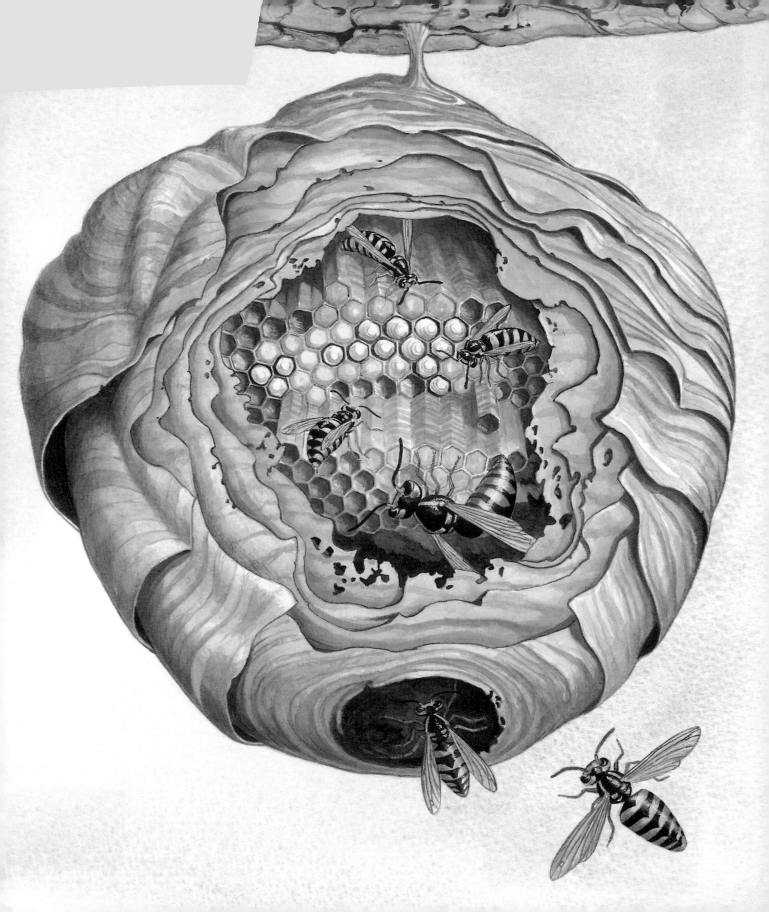

· CYCLES OF LIFE ·
Animal Builders

Written by David Stewart
Illustrated by Sean Milne
Created and designed by David Salariya

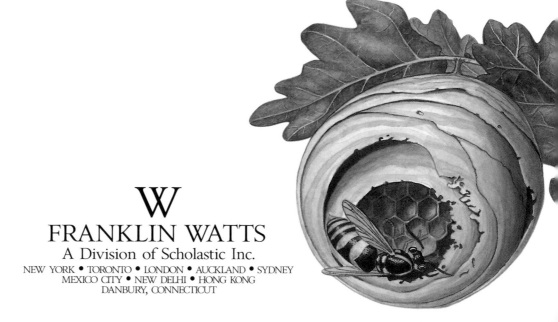

W
FRANKLIN WATTS
A Division of Scholastic Inc.
NEW YORK • TORONTO • LONDON • AUCKLAND • SYDNEY
MEXICO CITY • NEW DELHI • HONG KONG
DANBURY, CONNECTICUT

Contents

Introduction

Animals build shelters to protect themselves from heat, cold, rain, snow, and wind. Their shelters also give them a safe and warm place to bring up their babies.

Animals make different kinds of shelters. The type of shelter they build depends on where they live and what materials they can find to use.

In this book you will see how five different animals make different kinds of shelters.

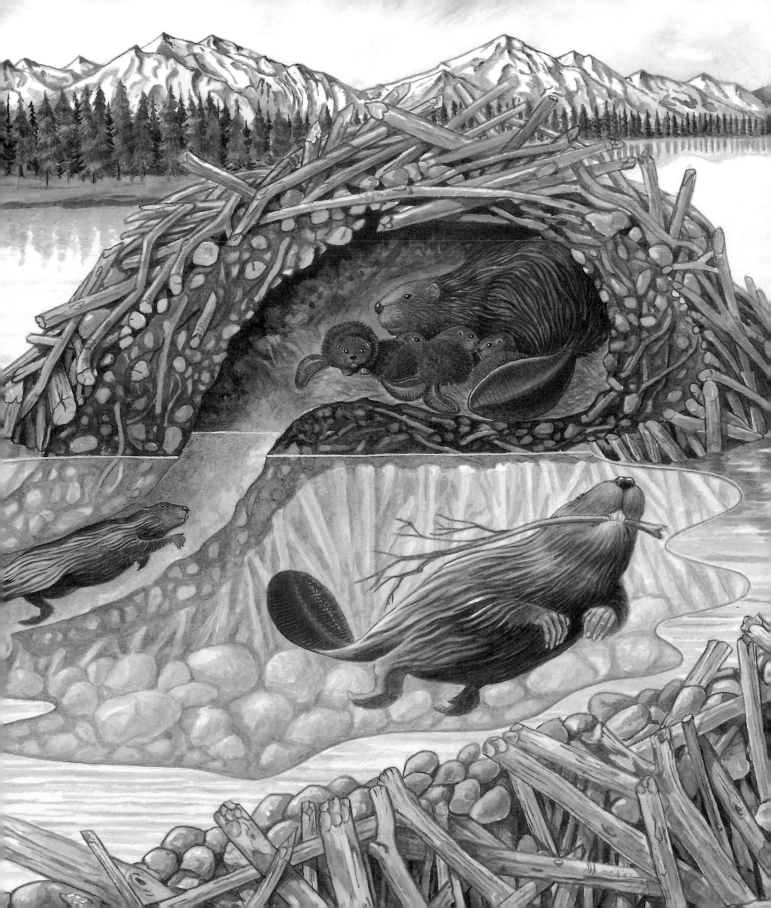

The Wasp Nest

Wasps are **insects**.
They live as a big family
inside the nest.

In spring, a female wasp,
called a **queen**, builds a
nest from wood pulp. Inside
the nest she builds a **comb**.
The comb is made up of
many **cells**. She lays eggs
in these cells. Wasps, called
workers, hatch
from them.

Workers

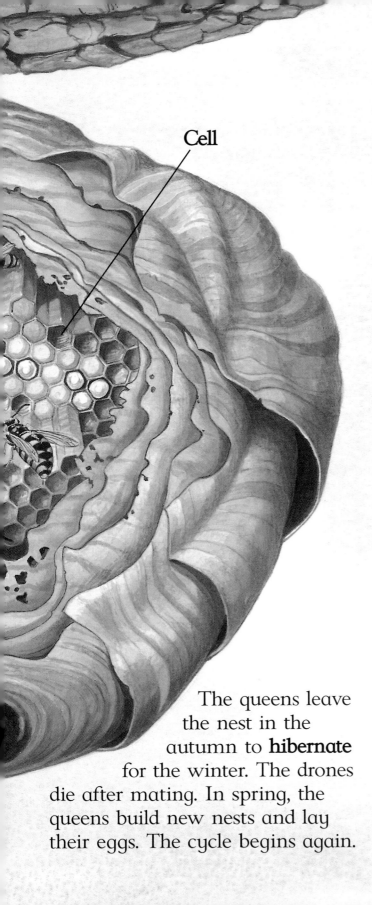

Cell

Once the workers have hatched, they take over building the cells that make up the nest.

Towards the end of summer, the queen lays larger eggs. These eggs contain new queens. She also lays eggs which contain male wasps, called **drones**. The drones and the new queens **mate**.

The queens leave the nest in the autumn to **hibernate** for the winter. The drones die after mating. In spring, the queens build new nests and lay their eggs. The cycle begins again.

The Weaver Bird Nest

These birds are called "weaver birds" because their nests look like they are woven.

In fact, the birds use their **beaks** and feet to loop, twist, and knot strips of leaves and grass.

Weaver bird

Young birds often make messy nests. As the birds practice more, their nests become neater and stronger.

12

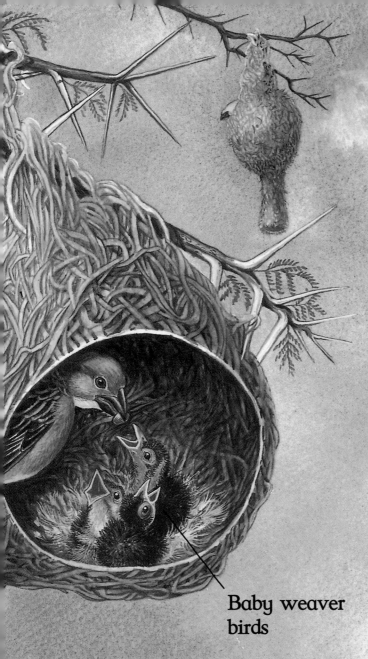

The male bird builds the nest. If a female thinks it's good enough, she lines it with feathers and lays her eggs.

The special hanging shape of the nest protects the eggs and baby birds from snakes and lizards.

Baby weaver birds

The parents feed the baby birds with seed. When they are old enough, they will fly and find their own food.

The Woodpecker Nest

Woodpeckers like to live near trees. These can be in woods or gardens.

A woodpecker pecks a hole in a tree trunk with its strong beak to make its nest.

The woodpecker also uses its beak to tap tree trunks in search of insects to eat.

Squirrel

16

The female woodpecker lays between four and seven eggs inside the hole.

The eggs hatch after 16 days. The baby birds are able to fly three weeks later.

The male and female woodpecker take turns sitting on the eggs in the nest and keep them warm.

Baby woodpeckers

The Beaver Lodge

Beavers are **mammals**. They live and work in small families.

After mating, the male and female beavers stay together the rest of their lives. They both help to build their home which is called a **lodge**.

Lodge made from sticks and mud

Beavers chew through tree branches with their huge, razor sharp teeth. These grow as fast as they are worn down.

The beavers live inside the lodge, which is called a **chamber**. This is above the water level.

They also build a **dam** nearby. This floods the area around the lodge. The entrance tunnel to the lodge can then be kept under water so that the young beavers are protected from other animals.

Baby beavers

Chamber

Dam

23

The Badger Sett

Badgers are mammals. They usually live in woodlands.

Badgers dig their homes under the ground. These are called setts. Each sett has at least two entrances and many tunnels and chambers.

Badgers will eat almost anything, including earthworms, mice, moles, frogs, snails, and wasps.

Entrance to sett

Badger cub

Badgers sleep during the day and look for food at night. This is why they are usually seen early in the morning or late at night.

Badger babies are called cubs. One to five cubs are born, usually in February. The cubs will remain with their parents until the autumn.

Animal Builders

All of these animals have built completely different types of shelters using different materials and building techniques.

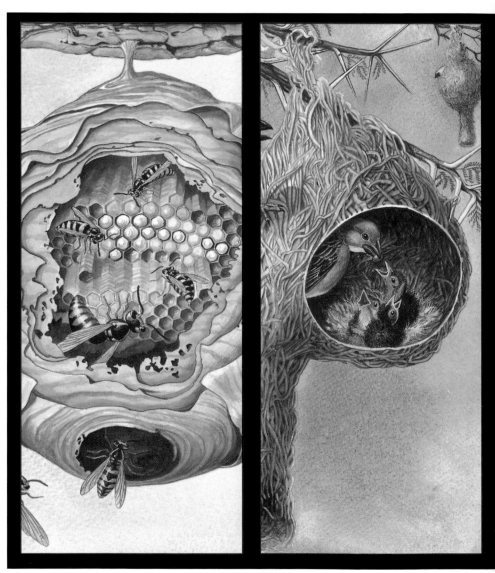

Paper Maker
The wasps' nest is made from a papery material. The wasps make this by mixing chewed wood with **saliva**.

Weaver
The weaver birds' nest is made from pieces of grass, which the birds knot and twist together.

Driller
The woodpeckers build their nest by pecking a hole in the trunk of a tree using their beaks.

Dam Builder
The beavers' lodge is made from sticks and mud. They also build a dam to flood the area around their lodge.

Burrower
Badgers build their setts underground by burrowing through the earth.

29

Animal Builders Words

Beak
The hard and pointed part around the mouth of a bird.

Cell
Parts of a wasps' nest in which eggs are laid and hatched. Each cell has eight sides and is made from paper.

Chamber
The living area of shelters made by animals such as beavers and badgers.

Comb
A group of many cells that all fit together inside a wasps' nest.

Dam
A type of wall built by beavers across a lake or river. Dams are made from sticks and they stop the flow of water.

Drones
Fertile male wasps; they mate with the queen wasps before dying in the autumn.

Hibernate
When animals spend the winter months sleeping for weeks on end in a nest or shelter.

Insect
An animal that has a hard outer covering and a body that is divided into three parts. Insects have six legs.

Lodge
The house that beavers build to live in. It is made from sticks and mud.

Mammal
A warm-blooded animal, that is usually covered with fur or hair.

Mate
When a male and female join together to have babies.

Queen wasp
The largest wasp in the nest. Her main job is to lay eggs. She is the mother of all the other wasps in the nest.

Saliva
A clear liquid in the mouth which helps animals chew and swallow food. Wasps use saliva to help them chew wood into a soft pulp.

Worker wasp
Female wasps that cannot lay eggs. Their main job is to feed the grubs in the nest, help build the nest, and look after the queen.

Index

31

Language Consultant:
Betty Root

Natural History Consultant:
Dr. Gerald Legg

Editors:
Stephanie Cole
Karen Barker Smith

Created, designed and produced by
The Salariya Book Company Ltd
Book House
25 Marlborough Place
Brighton BN1 1UB

Visit the Salariya Book Company at **www.salariya.com**

A catalog record for this title is available from
the Library of Congress.

ISBN 0-531-14662-6 (Lib. Bdg.)
ISBN 0-531-14839-4 (Pbk.)

Published in the United States in 2002 by Franklin Watts,
A Division of Scholastic Inc.
90 Sherman Turnpike
Danbury, CT 06816

Printed in China.